Caleb slipped his hand into mine as we stood on the porch, watching the road. He was afraid.

"Will she be nice?" he asked. "Like Maggie?"

"Sarah will be nice," I told him.

"How far away is Maine?" he asked.

"You know how far. Far away, by the sea."

"Will Sarah bring some sea?" he asked.

"No, you cannot bring the sea."

The sheep ran in the field, and far off the cows moved slowly to the pond, like turtles.

"Will she like us?" asked Caleb very softly.

I watched a marsh hawk wheel down behind the barn.

He looked up at me.

"Of course she will like us." He answered his own question. "We are nice," he added, making me smile.

ALSO BY
PATRICIA MACLACHLAN

WRITTEN WITH
EMILY MACLACHLAN CHAREST

*Painting the Wind*

*Bittle*

*Once I Ate a Pie*

*Fiona Loves the Night*

*I Didn't Do It*

*Before You Came*

*Cat Talk*

# PATRICIA MacLACHLAN

# Sarah, Plain and Tall

A CHARLOTTE ZOLOTOW BOOK

*An Imprint of HarperCollinsPublishers*

Sarah, Plain and Tall 30th Anniversary Edition

Library of Congress Cataloging-in-Publication Data
MacLachlan, Patricia.
Sarah, plain and tall.
p.    cm.
Summary: When their father invites a mail-order bride to come live with them in their
prairie home, Caleb and Anna are captivated by her and hope that she will stay.
ISBN 978-0-06-239952-6 (pbk.)
1. Children's stories, American. [1. Stepmothers—Fiction. 2. Frontier and pioneer
life—Fiction.] I. Title.
PZ7.M2225 Sar 1984                                                    83-49481
[Fic]                                                                       CIP
                                                                           AC

Revised paperback edition, 2015
❖
17  18  19   OPM   10  9  8  7  6

*For old friends, dear friends—*
DICK AND WENDY PUFF,
ALLISON AND DEREK

# Sarah, Plain and Tall

# 1

"Did Mama sing every day?" asked Caleb. "Every-single-day?" He sat close to the fire, his chin in his hand. It was dusk, and the dogs lay beside him on the warm hearthstones.

"Every-single-day," I told him for the second time this week. For the twentieth time this month. The hundredth time this year? And the past few years?

"And did Papa sing, too?"

"Yes. Papa sang, too. Don't get so close, Caleb. You'll heat up."

He pushed his chair back. It made a hol-
low scraping sound on the hearthstones, and
the dogs stirred. Lottie, small and black,
wagged her tail and lifted her head. Nick
slept on.

I turned the bread dough over and over
on the marble slab on the kitchen table.

"Well, Papa doesn't sing anymore," said
Caleb very softly. A log broke apart and
crackled in the fireplace. He looked up at
me. "What did I look like when I was born?"

"You didn't have any clothes on," I told
him.

"I know that," he said.

"You looked like this." I held the bread
dough up in a round pale ball.

"I had hair," said Caleb seriously.

"Not enough to talk about," I said.

"And she named me Caleb," he went on,
filling in the old familiar story.

"*I* would have named you Troublesome," I

said, making Caleb smile.

"And Mama handed me to you in the yellow blanket and said . . ." He waited for me to finish the story. "And said . . . ?"

I sighed. "And Mama said, 'Isn't he beautiful, Anna?'"

"And I was," Caleb finished.

Caleb thought the story was over, and I didn't tell him what I had really thought. He was homely and plain, and he had a terrible holler and a horrid smell. But these were not the worst of him. Mama died the next morning. That was the worst thing about Caleb.

"Isn't he beautiful, Anna?" Her last words to me. I had gone to bed thinking how wretched he looked. And I forgot to say good night.

I wiped my hands on my apron and went to the window. Outside, the prairie reached out and touched the places where the sky came down. Though winter was nearly over, there were patches of snow and ice everywhere. I looked at the long dirt road that crawled across the plains, remembering the morning that Mama had died, cruel and sunny. They had come for her in a wagon and taken her away to be buried. And then the cousins and aunts and uncles had come and tried to fill up the house. But they couldn't.

Slowly, one by one, they left. And then the days seemed long and dark like winter days, even though it wasn't winter. And Papa didn't sing.

*Isn't he beautiful, Anna?*

*No, Mama.*

It was hard to think of Caleb as beautiful. It took three whole days for me to love him, sitting in the chair by the fire, Papa washing up the supper dishes, Caleb's tiny hand brushing my cheek. And a smile. It was the smile, I know.

"Can you remember her songs?" asked

Caleb. "Mama's songs?"

I turned from the window. "No. Only that she sang about flowers and birds. Sometimes about the moon at nighttime."

Caleb reached down and touched Lottie's head.

"Maybe," he said, his voice low, "if you remember the songs, then I might remember her, too."

My eyes widened and tears came. Then the door opened and wind blew in with Papa, and I went to stir the stew. Papa put his arms around me and put his nose in my hair.

"Nice soapy smell, that stew," he said.

I laughed. "That's my hair."

Caleb came over and threw his arms around Papa's neck and hung down as Papa swung him back and forth, and the dogs sat up.

"Cold in town," said Papa. "And Jack was feisty." Jack was Papa's horse that he'd raised from a colt. "Rascal," murmured Papa, smiling, because no matter what Jack did Papa loved him.

I spooned up the stew and lighted the oil lamp and we ate with the dogs crowding under the table, hoping for spills or hand-outs.

Papa might not have told us about Sarah that night if Caleb hadn't asked him the question. After the dishes were cleared and washed and Papa was filling the tin pail with ashes, Caleb spoke up. It wasn't a question, really.

"You don't sing anymore," he said. He said it harshly. Not because he meant to, but because he had been thinking of it for so long. "Why?" he asked more gently.

Slowly Papa straightened up. There was a long silence, and the dogs looked up, won-dering at it.

"I've forgotten the old songs," said Papa quietly. He sat down. "But maybe there's a way to remember them." He looked up at us.

"How?" asked Caleb eagerly.

Papa leaned back in the chair. "I've placed an advertisement in the newspapers. For help."

"You mean a housekeeper?" I asked, surprised.

Caleb and I looked at each other and burst out laughing, remembering Hilly, our old housekeeper. She was round and slow and shuffling. She snored in a high whistle at night, like a teakettle, and let the fire go out.

"No," said Papa slowly. "Not a housekeeper." He paused. "A wife."

Caleb stared at Papa. "A wife? You mean a mother?"

Nick slid his face onto Papa's lap and Papa stroked his ears.

"That, too," said Papa. "Like Maggie."

Matthew, our neighbor to the south, had written to ask for a wife and mother for his children. And Maggie had come from Tennessee. Her hair was the color of turnips and she laughed.

Papa reached into his pocket and unfolded a letter written on white paper. "And I have received an answer." Papa read to us:

"Dear Mr. Jacob Witting,

"I am Sarah Wheaton from Maine as you will see from my letter. I am answering your advertisement. I have never been married, though I have been asked. I have lived with an older brother, William, who is about to be married. His wife-to-be is young and energetic.

"I have always loved to live by the sea, but at this time I feel a move is necessary. And the truth is, the sea is as far east as I can go. My choice, as you can see, is limited. This should not be taken as an insult. I am strong and I work hard and I am willing to travel. But I am not mild mannered. If you should still care to write, I would be interested in your children and about where you live. And you.

"Very truly yours,

"Sarah Elisabeth Wheaton

"P.S. Do you have opinions on cats? I have one."

No one spoke when Papa finished the letter. He kept looking at it in his hands, reading it over to himself. Finally I turned my head a bit to sneak a look at Caleb. He was smiling. I smiled too.

"One thing," I said in the quiet of the room.

"What's that?" asked Papa, looking up.

I put my arm around Caleb.

"Ask her if she sings," I said.

# 2

Caleb and Papa and I wrote letters to Sarah, and before the ice and snow had melted from the fields, we all received answers. Mine came first.

Dear Anna,

Yes, I can braid hair and I can make stew and bake bread, though I prefer to build bookshelves and paint.

My favorite colors are the colors of the sea, blue and gray and green, depending on the weather. My brother William is a fisherman, and he tells me that when he is in the middle of a fog-bound sea the water is a color for which there is no name. He catches flounder and sea bass and bluefish. Sometimes he sees whales. And birds, too, of course. I am enclosing a book of sea birds so you will see what William and I see every day.

Very truly yours,<br>Sarah Elisabeth Wheaton

Caleb read and read the letter so many times that the ink began to run and the folds tore. He read the book about sea birds over and over.

"Do you think she'll come?" asked Caleb. "And will she stay? What if she thinks we are loud and pesky?"

"You *are* loud and pesky," I told him. But I

was worried, too. Sarah loved the sea, I could tell. Maybe she wouldn't leave there after all to come where there were fields and grass and sky and not much else.

"What if she comes and doesn't like our house?" Caleb asked. "I told her it was small. Maybe I shouldn't have told her it was small."

"Hush, Caleb. Hush."

Caleb's letter came soon after, with a picture of a cat drawn on the envelope.

Dear Caleb,

My cat's name is Seal because she is gray like the seals that swim offshore in Maine. She is glad that Lottie and Nick send their greetings. She likes dogs most of the time. She says their footprints are much larger than hers (which she is enclosing in return).

Your house sounds lovely, even though it is far out in the country with no close neighbors. My house is tall and the shingles are gray because of the salt from the sea. There are roses nearby.

Yes, I do like small rooms sometimes. Yes, I can keep a fire going at night. I do not know if I snore. Seal has never told me.

Very truly yours,

Sarah Elisabeth

"Did you really ask her about fires and snoring?" I asked, amazed.

"I wished to know," Caleb said.

He kept the letter with him, reading it in the barn and in the fields and by the cow pond. And always in bed at night.

One morning, early, Papa and Caleb and I were cleaning out the horse stalls and putting down new bedding. Papa stopped suddenly and leaned on his pitchfork.

"Sarah has said she will come for a month's time if we wish her to," he said, his voice loud in the dark barn. "To see how it is. Just to see."

Caleb stood by the stall door and folded his arms across his chest.

"I think," he began. Then, "I think," he said slowly, "that it would be good—to say yes," he finished in a rush.

Papa looked at me.

"I say yes," I told him, grinning.

"Yes," said Papa. "Then yes it is."

And the three of us, all smiling, went to work again.

The next day Papa went to town to mail his letter to Sarah. It was rainy for days, and the clouds followed. The house was cool and damp and quiet. Once I set four places at the table, then caught myself and put the extra plate away. Three lambs were born, one with a black face. And then Papa's letter came. It was very short.

Dear Jacob,

I will come by train. I will wear a yellow bonnet. I am plain and tall.

Sarah


"What's that?" asked Caleb excitedly, peering over Papa's shoulder. He pointed. "There, written at the bottom of the letter."

Papa read it to himself. Then he smiled, holding up the letter for us to see.

*Tell them I sing* was all it said.

# 3

Sarah came in the spring. She came through green grass fields that bloomed with Indian paintbrush, red and orange, and blue-eyed grass.

Papa got up early for the long day's trip to the train and back. He brushed his hair so slick and shiny that Caleb laughed. He wore a clean blue shirt, and a belt instead of suspenders.

He fed and watered the horses, talking to them as he hitched them up to the wagon. Old Bess, calm and kind; Jack, wild-eyed, reaching over to nip Bess on the neck.

"Clear day, Bess," said Papa, rubbing her nose.

"Settle down, Jack." He leaned his head on Jack.

And then Papa drove off along the dirt road to fetch Sarah. Papa's new wife. Maybe. Maybe our new mother.

Gophers ran back and forth across the road, stopping to stand up and watch the wagon. Far off in a field a woodchuck ate and listened. Ate and listened.

Caleb and I did our chores without talking. We shoveled out the stalls and laid down new hay. We fed the sheep. We swept and straightened and carried wood and water. And then our chores were done.

Caleb pulled on my shirt.

"Is my face clean?" he asked. "Can my face be *too* clean?" He looked alarmed.

"No, your face is clean but not too clean," I said.

Caleb slipped his hand into mine as we stood on the porch, watching the road. He was afraid.

"Will she be nice?" he asked. "Like Maggie?"

"Sarah will be nice," I told him.

"How far away is Maine?" he asked.

"You know how far. Far away, by the sea."

"Will Sarah bring some sea?" he asked.

"No, you cannot bring the sea."

The sheep ran in the field, and far off the cows moved slowly to the pond, like turtles.

"Will she like us?" asked Caleb very softly.

I watched a marsh hawk wheel down behind the barn.

He looked up at me.

"Of course she will like us." He answered his own question. "We are nice," he added, making me smile.

We waited and watched. I rocked on the porch and Caleb rolled a marble on the wood floor. Back and forth. Back and forth. The marble was blue.

We saw the dust from the wagon first, rising above the road, above the heads of Jack and Old Bess. Caleb climbed up onto the porch roof and shaded his eyes.

"A bonnet!" he cried. "I see a yellow bonnet!"

The dogs came out from under the porch, ears up, their eyes on the cloud of dust bringing Sarah. The wagon passed the fenced field, and the cows and sheep looked up, too. It rounded the windmill and the barn and the windbreak of Russian olive that Mama had planted long ago. Nick began to bark, then Lottie, and the wagon clattered into the yard and stopped by the steps.

"Hush," said Papa to the dogs.

And it was quiet.

Sarah stepped down from the wagon, a cloth bag in her hand. She reached up and took off her yellow bonnet, smoothing back her brown hair into a bun. She was plain and tall.

"Did you bring some sea?" cried Caleb beside me.

"Something from the sea," said Sarah, smiling. "And me." She turned and lifted a black case from the wagon. "And Seal, too."

Carefully she opened the case, and Seal, gray with white feet, stepped out. Lottie lay down, her head on her paws, staring. Nick leaned down to sniff. Then he lay down, too.

"The cat will be good in the barn," said Papa. "For mice."

Sarah smiled. "She will be good in the house, too."

Sarah took Caleb's hand, then mine. Her hands were large and rough. She gave Caleb a shell—a moon snail, she called it—that was curled and smelled of salt.

"The gulls fly high and drop the shells on the rocks below," she told Caleb. "When the shell is broken, they eat what is inside."

"That is very smart," said Caleb.

"For you, Anna," said Sarah, "a sea stone."

And she gave me the smoothest and whitest stone I had ever seen.

"The sea washes over and over and around the stone, rolling it until it is round and perfect."

"That is very smart, too," said Caleb. He looked up at Sarah. "We do not have the sea here."

Sarah turned and looked out over the plains.

"No," she said. "There is no sea here. But the land rolls a little like the sea."

My father did not see her look, but I did. And I knew that Caleb had seen it, too. Sarah was not smiling. Sarah was already lonely. In a month's time the preacher might come to marry Sarah and Papa. And a month was a long time. Time enough for her to change her mind and leave us.

Papa took Sarah's bags inside, where her room was ready with a quilt on the bed and blue flax dried in a vase on the night table.

Seal stretched and made a small cat sound. I watched her circle the dogs and sniff the air. Caleb came out and stood beside me.

"When will we sing?" he whispered.

I shook my head, turning the white stone over and over in my hand. I wished everything was as perfect as the stone. I wished that Papa and Caleb and I were perfect for Sarah. I wished we had a sea of our own.

# 4

The dogs loved Sarah first. Lottie slept beside her bed, curled in a soft circle, and Nick leaned his face on the covers in the morning, watching for the first sign that Sarah was awake. No one knew where Seal slept. Seal was a roamer.

Sarah's collection of shells sat on the windowsill.

"A scallop," she told us, picking up the shells one by one, "a sea clam, an oyster, a razor clam. And a conch shell. If you put it to your ear you can hear the sea." She put it to

Caleb's ear, then mine. Papa listened, too. Then Sarah listened once more, with a look so sad and far away that Caleb leaned against me.

"At least Sarah can hear the sea," he whispered.

Papa was quiet and shy with Sarah, and so was I. But Caleb talked to Sarah from morning until the light left the sky.

"Where are you going?" he asked. "To do what?"

"To pick flowers," said Sarah. "I'll hang some of them upside down and dry them so they'll keep some color. And we can have flowers all winter long."

"I'll come, too!" cried Caleb. "Sarah said winter," he said to me. "That means Sarah will stay."

Together we picked flowers, paintbrush and clover and prairie violets. There were buds on the wild roses that climbed up the paddock fence.

"The roses will bloom in early summer," I told Sarah. I looked to see if she knew what I was thinking. Summer was when the wedding would be. *Might* be. Sarah and Papa's wedding.

We hung the flowers from the ceiling in little bunches. "I've never seen this before," said Sarah. "What is it called?"

"Bride's bonnet," I told her.

Caleb smiled at the name.

"We don't have this by the sea," she said. "We have seaside goldenrod and wild asters and woolly ragwort."

"Woolly ragwort!" Caleb whooped. He made up a song.

> *"Woolly ragwort all around,*
> *Woolly ragwort on the ground,*
> *Woolly ragwort grows and grows,*
> *Woolly ragwort in your nose."*

Sarah and Papa laughed, and the dogs lifted their heads and thumped their tails against the wood floor. Seal sat on a kitchen chair and watched us with yellow eyes.

We ate Sarah's stew, the late light coming through the windows. Papa had baked bread that was still warm from the fire.

"The stew is fine," said Papa.

"Ayuh." Sarah nodded. "The bread, too."

"What does 'ayuh' mean?" asked Caleb.

"In Maine it means yes," said Sarah. "Do you want more stew?"

"Ayuh," said Caleb.

"Ayuh," echoed my father.

After dinner Sarah told us about William. "He has a gray-and-white boat named *Kittiwake*." She looked out the window. "That is a small gull found way off the shore where William fishes. There are three aunts who live near us. They wear silk dresses and no shoes. You would love them."

"Ayuh," said Caleb.

"Does your brother look like you?" I asked.

"Yes," said Sarah. "He is plain and tall."

At dusk Sarah cut Caleb's hair on the front steps, gathering his curls and scattering them on the fence and ground. Seal batted some hair around the porch as the dogs watched.

"Why?" asked Caleb.

"For the birds," said Sarah. "They will use it for their nests. Later we can look for nests of curls."

"Sarah said 'later,'" Caleb whispered to me as we spread his hair about. "Sarah will stay."

Sarah cut Papa's hair, too. No one else saw, but I found him behind the barn, tossing the pieces of hair into the wind for the birds.

Sarah brushed my hair and tied it up in back with a rose velvet ribbon she had brought from Maine. She brushed hers long and free and tied it back, too, and we stood side by side looking into the mirror. I looked taller, like Sarah, and fair and thin. And with my hair pulled back I looked a little like her daughter. Sarah's daughter.

And then it was time for singing.

Sarah sang us a song we had never heard before as we sat on the porch, insects buzzing in the dark, the rustle of cows in the grasses. It was called "Sumer Is Icumen in," and she taught it to us all, even Papa, who sang as if he had never stopped singing.

> *"Sumer is icumen in,*
> *Lhude sing cuccu!"*

"What is sumer?" asked Caleb. He said it "soomer," the way Sarah had said it.

"Summer," said Papa and Sarah at the same time. Caleb and I looked at each other. Summer was coming.

"Tomorrow," said Sarah, "I want to see the

sheep. You know, I've never touched one."

"Never?" Caleb sat up.

"Never," said Sarah. She smiled and leaned back in her chair. "But I've touched seals. Real seals. They are cool and slippery and they slide through the water like fish. They can cry and sing. And sometimes they bark, a little like dogs."

Sarah barked like a seal. And Lottie and Nick came running from the barn to jump up on Sarah and lick her face and make her laugh. Sarah stroked them and scratched their ears and it was quiet again.

"I wish I could touch a seal right now," said Caleb, his voice soft in the night.

"So do I," said Sarah. She sighed, then she began to sing the summer song again. Far off in a field, a meadowlark sang, too.

# 5

The sheep made Sarah smile. She sank her fingers into their thick, coarse wool. She talked to them, running with the lambs, letting them suck on her fingers. She named them after her favorite aunts, Harriet and Mattie and Lou. She lay down in the field beside them and sang "Sumer Is Icumen in," her voice drifting over the meadow grasses, carried by the wind.

She cried when we found a lamb that had died, and she shouted and shook her fist at the turkey buzzards that came from nowhere to eat it. She would not let Caleb or me come near. And that night, Papa went with a shovel to bury the sheep and a lantern to bring Sarah back. She sat on the porch alone. Nick crept up to lean against her knees.

After dinner, Sarah drew pictures to send home to Maine. She began a charcoal drawing of the fields, rolling like the sea rolled. She drew a sheep whose ears were too big. And she drew a windmill.

"Windmill was my first word," said Caleb. "Papa told me so."

"Mine was flower," I said. "What was yours, Sarah?"

"Dune," said Sarah.

"Dune?" Caleb looked up.

"In Maine," said Sarah, "there are rock cliffs that rise up at the edge of the sea. And there are hills covered with pine and spruce trees, green with needles. But William and I found a sand dune all our own. It was soft and sparkling with bits of mica, and when we were little we would slide down the dune into the water."

Caleb looked out the window.

"We have no dunes here," he said.

Papa stood up.

"Yes we do," he said. He took the lantern and went out the door to the barn.

"We do?" Caleb called after him.

He ran ahead, Sarah and I following, the dogs close behind.

Next to the barn was Papa's mound of hay for bedding, nearly as tall as the barn, covered with canvas to keep the rain from rotting it. Papa carried the wooden ladder from the barn and leaned it against the hay.

"There." He smiled at Sarah. "Our dune."

Sarah was very quiet. The dogs looked up at her, waiting. Seal brushed against her legs, her tail in the air. Caleb reached over and took her hand.

"It looks high up," he said. "Are you scared, Sarah?"

"Scared? Scared!" exclaimed Sarah. "You bet I'm not scared."

She climbed the ladder, and Nick began to bark. She climbed to the very top of the hay and sat, looking down at us. Above, the stars were coming out. Papa piled a bed of loose hay below with his pitchfork. The light of the lantern made his eyes shine when he smiled up at Sarah.

"Fine?" called Papa.

"Fine," said Sarah. She lifted her arms over her head and slid down, down, into the soft hay. She lay, laughing, as the dogs rolled beside her.

"Was it a good dune?" called Caleb.

"Yes," said Sarah. "It is a fine dune."

Caleb and I climbed up and slid down. And Sarah did it three more times. At last Papa slid down, too, as the sky grew darker and the stars blinked like fireflies. We were covered with hay and dust, and we sneezed.

In the kitchen, Caleb and I washed in the big wooden tub and Sarah drew more pictures to send to William. One was of Papa, his hair curly and full of hay. She drew Caleb, sliding down the hay, his arms like Sarah's over his head. And she drew a picture of me in the tub, my hair long and straight and wet. She looked at her drawing of the fields for a long time.

"Something is missing," she told Caleb. "Something." And she put it away.

"'Dear William,'" Sarah read to us by lantern light that night. "'Sliding down our dune of hay is almost as fine as sliding down the sand dunes into the sea.'"

Caleb smiled at me across the table. He said nothing, but his mouth formed the words I had heard, too. *Our dune.*

# 6

The days grew longer. The cows moved close to the pond, where the water was cool and there were trees.

Papa taught Sarah how to plow the fields, guiding the plow behind Jack and Old Bess, the reins around her neck. When the chores were done we sat in the meadow with the sheep, Sarah beside us, watching Papa finish.

"Tell me about winter," said Sarah.

Old Bess nodded her head as she walked, but we could hear Papa speak sharply to Jack.

"Jack doesn't like work," said Caleb. "He

wants to be here in the sweet grass with us."

"I don't blame him," said Sarah. She lay back in the grass with her arms under her head. "Tell me about winter," she said again.

"Winter is cold here," said Caleb, and Sarah and I laughed.

"Winter is cold everywhere," I said.

"We go to school in winter," said Caleb. "Sums and writing and books," he sang.

"I am good at sums and writing," said Sarah. "I love books. How do you get to school?"

"Papa drives us in the wagon. Or we walk the three miles when there is not too much snow."

Sarah sat up. "Do you have lots of snow?"

"Lots and lots and lots of snow," chanted Caleb, rolling around in the grass. "Sometimes we have to dig our way out to feed the animals."

"In Maine the barns are attached to the

houses sometimes," said Sarah.

Caleb grinned. "So you could have a cow to Sunday supper?"

Sarah and I laughed.

"When there are bad storms, Papa ties a rope from the house to the barn so no one will get lost," said Caleb.

I frowned. I loved winter.

"There is ice on the windows on winter mornings," I told Sarah. "We can draw sparkling pictures and we can see our breath in the air. Papa builds a warm fire, and we bake hot biscuits and put on hundreds of sweaters. And if the snow is too high, we stay home from school and make snow people."

Sarah lay back in the tall grasses again, her face nearly hidden.

"And is there wind?" she asked.

"Do you like wind?" asked Caleb.

"There is wind by the sea," said Sarah.

"There is wind here," said Caleb happily.

"It blows the snow and brings tumbleweeds and makes the sheep run. Wind and wind and wind!" Caleb stood up and ran like the wind, and the sheep ran after him. Sarah and I watched him jump over rocks and gullies, the sheep behind him, stiff legged and fast. He circled the field, the sun making the top of his hair golden. He collapsed next to Sarah, and the lambs pushed their wet noses into us.

"Hello, Lou," said Sarah, smiling. "Hello, Mattie."

The sun rose higher, and Papa stopped to take off his hat and wipe his face with his sleeve.

"I'm hot," said Sarah. "I can't wait for winter wind. Let's swim."

"Swim where?" I asked her.

"I can't swim," said Caleb.

"Can't swim!" exclaimed Sarah. "I'll teach you in the cow pond."

"That's for cows!" I cried.

But Sarah had grabbed our hands and we were running through the fields, ducking under the fence to the far pond.

"Shoo, cows," said Sarah as the cows looked up, startled. She took off her dress and waded into the water in her petticoat. She dived suddenly and disappeared for a moment as Caleb and I watched. She came up, laughing, her hair streaming free. Water beads sat on her shoulders.

She tried to teach us how to float. I sank like a bucket filled with water and came up sputtering. But Caleb lay on his back and learned how to blow streams of water high in the air like a whale. The cows stood on the banks of the pond and stared and stopped their chewing. Water bugs circled us.

"Is this like the sea?" asked Caleb.

Sarah treaded water.

"The sea is salt," said Sarah. "It stretches out as far as you can see. It gleams like the sun on glass. There are waves."

"Like this?" asked Caleb, and he pushed a wave at Sarah, making her cough and laugh.

"Yes," she said. "Like that."

I held my breath and floated at last, looking up into the sky, afraid to speak. Crows flew over, three in a row. And I could hear a killdeer in the field.

We climbed the bank and dried ourselves and lay in the grass again. The cows watched, their eyes sad in their dinner-plate faces. And I slept, dreaming a perfect dream. The fields had turned to a sea that gleamed like sun on glass. And Sarah was happy.

# 7

The dandelions in the fields had gone by, their heads soft as feathers. The summer roses were opening.

Our neighbors, Matthew and Maggie, came to help Papa plow up a new field for corn. Sarah stood with us on the porch, watching their wagon wind up the road, two horses pulling it and one tied in back. I remembered the last time we had stood here alone, Caleb and I, waiting for Sarah.

Sarah's hair was in thick braids that circled her head, wild daisies tucked here and there. Papa had picked them for her.

Old Bess and Jack ran along the inside of the fence, whickering at the new horses.

"Papa needs five horses for the big gang plow," Caleb told Sarah. "Prairie grass is hard."

Matthew and Maggie came with their two children and a sackful of chickens. Maggie emptied the sack into the yard and three red banty chickens clucked and scattered.

"They are for you," she told Sarah. "For eating."

Sarah loved the chickens. She clucked back to them and fed them grain. They followed her, shuffling and scratching primly in the dirt. I knew they would not be for eating.

The children were young and named Rose and Violet, after flowers. They hooted and laughed and chased the chickens, who flew up to the porch roof, then the dogs, who crept quietly under the porch. Seal had long ago fled to the barn to sleep in cool hay.

Sarah and Maggie helped hitch the horses to the plow, then they set up a big table in the shade of the barn, covering it with a quilt and a kettle of flowers in the middle. They sat on the porch while Caleb and Matthew and Papa began their morning of plowing. I mixed biscuit dough just inside the door, watching.

"You are lonely, yes?" asked Maggie in her soft voice.

Sarah's eyes filled with tears. Slowly I stirred the dough.

Maggie reached over and took Sarah's hand.

"I miss the hills of Tennessee sometimes," she said.

Do not miss the hills, Maggie, I thought.

"I miss the sea," said Sarah.

*Do not miss the hills. Do not miss the sea.*

I stirred and stirred the dough.

"I miss my brother William," said Sarah. "But he is married. The house is hers now. Not mine any longer. There are three old aunts who all squawk together like crows at dawn. I miss them, too."

"There are always things to miss," said Maggie. "No matter where you are."

I looked out and saw Papa and Matthew and Caleb working. Rose and Violet ran in the fields. I felt something brush my legs and looked down at Nick, wagging his tail.

"I would miss you, Nick," I whispered. "I would." I knelt down and scratched his ears. "I miss Mama."

"I nearly forgot," said Maggie on the porch. "I have something more for you."

I carried the bowl outside and watched Maggie lift a low wooden box out of the wagon.

"Plants," she said to Sarah. "For your garden."

"My garden?" Sarah bent down to touch the plants.

"Zinnias and marigolds and wild fever-few," said Maggie. "You must have a garden. Wherever you are."

Sarah smiled. "I had a garden in Maine with dahlias and columbine. And nasturtiums the color of the sun when it sets. I don't know if nasturtiums would grow here."

"Try," said Maggie. "You must have a garden."

We planted the flowers by the porch, turning over the soil and patting it around them, and watering. Lottie and Nick came to sniff, and the chickens walked in the dirt, leaving prints. In the fields, the horses pulled the plow up and down under the hot summer sun.

Maggie wiped her face, leaving a streak of dirt.

"Soon you can drive your wagon over to

my house and I will give you more. I have tansy."

Sarah frowned. "I have never driven a wagon."

"I can teach you," said Maggie. "And so can Anna and Caleb. And Jacob."

Sarah turned to me.

"Can you?" she asked. "Can you drive a wagon?"

I nodded.

"And Caleb?"

"Yes."

"In Maine," said Sarah, "I would walk to town."

"Here it is different," said Maggie. "Here you will drive."

Way off in the sky, clouds gathered. Matthew and Papa and Caleb came in from the fields, their work done. We all ate in the shade.

"We are glad you are here," said Matthew

to Sarah. "A new friend. Maggie misses her friends sometimes."

Sarah nodded. "There is always something to miss, no matter where you are," she said, smiling at Maggie.

Rose and Violet fell asleep in the grass, their bellies full of meat and greens and biscuits. And when it was time to go, Papa and Matthew lifted them into the wagon to sleep on blankets.

Sarah walked slowly behind the wagon for a long time, waving, watching it disappear. Caleb and I ran to bring her back, the chickens running wildly behind us.

"What shall we name them?" asked Sarah, laughing as the chickens followed us into the house.

I smiled. I was right. The chickens would not be for eating.

And then Papa came, just before the rain, bringing Sarah the first roses of summer.

# 8

The rain came and passed, but strange clouds hung in the northwest, low and black and green. And the air grew still.

In the morning, Sarah dressed in a pair of overalls and went to the barn to have an argument with Papa. She took apples for Old Bess and Jack.

"Women don't wear overalls," said Caleb, running along behind her like one of Sarah's chickens.

"This woman does," said Sarah crisply.

Papa stood by the fence.

"I want to learn how to ride a horse," Sarah told him. "And then I want to learn how to drive the wagon. By myself."

Jack leaned over and nipped at Sarah's overalls. She fed him an apple. Caleb and I stood behind Sarah.

"I can ride a horse, I know," said Sarah. "I rode once when I was twelve. I will ride Jack." Jack was Sarah's favorite.

Papa shook his head. "Not Jack," he said. "Jack is sly."

"I am sly, too," said Sarah stubbornly.

Papa smiled. "Ayuh," he said, nodding. "But not Jack."

"Yes, Jack!" Sarah's voice was very loud.

"I can teach you how to drive a wagon. I have already taught you how to plow."

"And then I can go to town. By myself."

"Say no, Papa," Caleb whispered beside me.

"That's a fair thing, Sarah," said Papa. "We'll practice."

A soft rumble of thunder sounded. Papa looked up at the clouds.

"Today?" Can we begin today?" asked Sarah.

"Tomorrow is best," said Papa, looking worried. "I have to fix the house roof. A portion of it is loose. And there's a storm coming."

"We," said Sarah.

"What?" Papa turned.

"*We* will fix the roof," said Sarah. "I've done it before. I know about roofs. I am a good carpenter. Remember, I told you?"

There was thunder again, and Papa went to get the ladder.

"Are you fast?" he asked Sarah.

"I am fast and I am good," said Sarah. And they climbed the ladder to the roof, Sarah with wisps of hair around her face, her mouth full of nails, overalls like Papa's. Overalls that *were* Papa's.

Caleb and I went inside to close the

windows. We could hear the steady sound of hammers pounding the roof overhead.

"Why does she want to go to town by herself?" asked Caleb. "To leave us?"

I shook my head, weary with Caleb's questions. Tears gathered at the corners of my eyes. But there was no time to cry, for suddenly Papa called out.

"Caleb! Anna!"

We ran outside and saw a huge cloud, horribly black, moving toward us over the north fields. Papa slid down the roof, helping Sarah after him.

"A squall!" he yelled to us. He held up his arms and Sarah jumped off the porch roof.

"Get the horses inside," he ordered Caleb. "Get the sheep, Anna. And the cows. The barn is safest."

The grasses flattened. There was a hiss of wind, a sudden pungent smell. Our faces looked yellow in the strange light. Caleb and

I jumped over the fence and found the animals huddled by the barn. I counted the sheep to make sure they were all there, and herded them into a large stall. A few raindrops came, gentle at first, then stronger and louder, so that Caleb and I covered our ears and stared at each other without speaking. Caleb looked frightened and I tried to smile at him. Sarah carried a sack into the barn, her hair wet and streaming down her neck, Papa came behind, Lottie and Nick with him, their ears flat against their heads.

"Wait!" cried Sarah. "My chickens!"

"No, Sarah!" Papa called after her. But Sarah had already run from the barn into a sheet of rain. My father followed her. The sheep nosed open their stall door and milled around the barn, bleating. Nick crept under my arm, and a lamb, Mattie with the black face, stood close to me, trembling. There was a soft paw on my lap, then a gray body. Seal.

And then, as the thunder pounded and the wind rose and there was the terrible crackling of lightning close by, Sarah and Papa stood in the barn doorway, wet to the skin. Papa carried Sarah's chickens. Sarah came with an armful of summer roses.

Sarah's chickens were not afraid, and they settled like small red bundles in the hay. Papa closed the door at last, shutting out some of the sounds of the storm. The barn was eerie and half lighted, like dusk without a lantern. Papa spread blankets around our shoulders and Sarah unpacked a bag of cheese and bread and jam. At the very bottom of the bag were Sarah's shells.

Caleb got up and went over to the small barn window.

"What color is the sea when it storms?" he asked Sarah.

"Blue," said Sarah, brushing her wet hair back with her fingers. "And gray and green."

Caleb nodded and smiled.

"Look," he said to her. "Look what is missing from your drawing."

Sarah went to stand between Caleb and Papa by the window. She looked a long time without speaking. Finally, she touched Papa's shoulder.

"We have squalls in Maine, too," she said. "Just like this. It will be all right, Jacob."

Papa said nothing. But he put his arm around her, and leaned over to rest his chin in her hair. I closed my eyes, suddenly remembering Mama and Papa standing that way, Mama smaller than Sarah, her hair fair against Papa's shoulder. When I opened my eyes again, it was Sarah standing there. Caleb looked at me and smiled and smiled until he could smile no more.

We slept in the hay all night, waking when the wind was wild, sleeping again when it was quiet. And at dawn there was the sudden sound of hail, like stones tossed against the barn. We stared out the window, watching the ice marbles bounce on the ground. And when it was over we opened the barn door and walked out into the early-morning light. The hail crunched and melted beneath our feet. It was white and gleaming for as far as we looked, like sun on glass. Like the sea.

# 9

It was very quiet. The dogs leaned down to eat the hailstones. Seal stepped around them and leaped up on the fence to groom herself. A tree had blown over near the cow pond. And the wild roses were scattered on the ground, as if a wedding had come and gone there. "I'm glad I saved an armful" was all that Sarah said.

Only one field was badly damaged, and Sarah and Papa hitched up the horses and plowed and replanted during the next two days. The roof had held.

"I told you I know about roofs," Sarah told Papa, making him smile.

Papa kept his promise to Sarah. When the work was done, he took her out into the fields, Papa riding Jack who was sly, and Sarah riding Old Bess. Sarah was quick to learn.

"Too quick," Caleb complained to me as we watched from the fence. He thought a moment. "Maybe she'll fall off and have to stay here. Why?" he asked, turning to me. "Why does she have to go away alone?"

"Hush up, Caleb," I said crossly. "Hush up."

"I could get sick and make her stay here," said Caleb.

"No."

"We could tie her up."

"No."

And Caleb began to cry, and I took him inside the barn where we could both cry.

Papa and Sarah came to hitch the horses

to the wagon, so Sarah could practice driving. Papa didn't see Caleb's tears, and he sent him with an ax to begin chopping up the tree by the pond for firewood. I stood and watched Sarah, the reins in her hands, Papa next to her in the wagon. I could see Caleb standing by the pond, one hand shading his eyes, watching, too. I went into the safe darkness of the barn then, Sarah's chickens scuttling along behind me.

"Why?" I asked out loud, echoing Caleb's question.

The chickens watched me, their eyes small and bright.

The next morning Sarah got up early and put on her blue dress. She took apples to the barn. She loaded a bundle of hay on the wagon for Old Bess and Jack. She put on her yellow bonnet.

"Remember Jack," said Papa. "A strong hand."

"Yes, Jacob."

"Best to be home before dark," said Papa. "Driving a wagon is hard if there's no full moon."

"Yes, Jacob."

Sarah kissed us all, even my father, who looked surprised.

"Take care of Seal," she said to Caleb and me. And with a whisper to Old Bess and a stern word to Jack, Sarah climbed up in the wagon and drove away.

"Very good," murmured Papa as he watched. And after a while he turned and went out into the fields.

Caleb and I watched Sarah from the porch. Caleb took my hand, and the dogs lay down beside us. It was sunny, and I remembered another time when a wagon had taken Mama away. It had been a day just like this day. And Mama had never come back.

Seal jumped up to the porch, her feet

making a small thump. Caleb leaned down and picked her up and walked inside. I took the broom and slowly swept the porch. Then I watered Sarah's plants. Caleb cleaned out the wood stove and carried the ashes to the barn, spilling them so that I had to sweep the porch again.

"I *am* loud and pesky," Caleb cried suddenly. "You said so! And she has gone to buy a train ticket to go away!"

"No, Caleb. She would tell us."

"The house is too small," said Caleb. "That's what it is."

"The house is not too small," I said.

I looked at Sarah's drawing of the fields pinned up on the wall next to the window.

"What is missing?" I asked Caleb. "You said you knew what was missing."

"Colors," said Caleb wearily. "The colors of the sea."

Outside, clouds moved into the sky and

went away again. We took lunch to Papa, cheese and bread and lemonade. Caleb nudged me.

"Ask him. Ask Papa."

"What has Sarah gone to do?" I asked.

"I don't know," said Papa. He squinted at me. Then he sighed and put one hand on Caleb's head, one on mine. "Sarah is Sarah. She does things her way, you know."

"I know," said Caleb very softly.

Papa picked up his shovel and put on his hat.

"Ask if she's coming back," whispered Caleb.

"Of course she's coming back," I said. "Seal is here." But I would not ask the question. I was afraid to hear the answer.

We fed the sheep, and I set the table for dinner. Four plates. The sun dropped low over the west fields. Lottie and Nick stood at the door, wagging their tails, asking for supper.

Papa came to light the stove. And then it was dusk. Soon it would be dark. Caleb sat on the porch steps, turning his moon snail shell over and over in his hand. Seal brushed back and forth against him.

Suddenly Lottie began to bark, and Nick jumped off the porch and ran down the road.

"Dust!" cried Caleb. He climbed the porch and stood on the roof. "Dust, and a yellow bonnet!"

Slowly the wagon came around the windmill and the barn and the windbreak and into the yard, the dogs jumping happily beside it.

"Hush, dogs," said Sarah. And Nick leaped up into the wagon to sit by Sarah.

Papa took the reins and Sarah climbed down from the wagon.

Caleb burst into tears.

"Seal was very worried!" he cried.

Sarah put her arms around him, and he

wailed into her dress. "And the house is too small, we thought! And I am loud and pesky!"

Sarah looked at Papa and me over Caleb's head.

"We thought you might be thinking of leaving us," I told her. "Because you miss the sea."

Sarah smiled.

"No," she said. "I will always miss my old home, but the truth of it is I would miss you more."

Papa smiled at Sarah, then he bent quickly to unhitch the horses from the wagon. He led them to the barn for water.

Sarah handed me a package.

"For Anna," she said. "And Caleb. For all of us."

The package was small, wrapped in brown paper with a rubber band around it. Very carefully I unwrapped it, Caleb peering closely. Inside were three colored pencils.

"Blue," said Caleb slowly, "and gray. And green."

Sarah nodded.

Suddenly Caleb grinned.

"Papa," he called. "Papa, come quickly! Sarah has brought the sea!"

*We eat our night meal by candlelight, the four of us. Sarah has brought candles from town. And nasturtium seeds for her garden, and a book of songs to teach us. It is late, and Caleb is nearly sleeping by his plate and Sarah is smiling at my father. Soon there will be a wedding. Papa says that when the preacher asks if he will have Sarah for his wife, he will answer, "Ayuh."*

*Autumn will come, then winter, cold with a wind that blows like the wind off the sea in Maine. There will be nests of curls to look for, and dried flowers all winter long. When there are storms, Papa will stretch a rope from the door to the barn so we will not be lost* when we feed the sheep and the cows and Jack and Old Bess. And Sarah's chickens, if they aren't living in the house. There will be Sarah's sea, blue and gray and green, hanging on the wall. And songs, old ones and new. And Seal with yellow eyes. And there will be Sarah, plain and tall.

# Sarah, Plain and Tall
## 30TH ANNIVERSARY
## Bonus Materials

*Patricia MacLachlan: Newbery Medal
Acceptance Speech*

*Discussion Guide*

*Suggested Reading List*

# Newbery Medal Acceptance
## By Patricia MacLachlan

There should be words more eloquent than *thank you*, words that communicate the great satisfaction I feel that the Newbery Committee has chosen *Sarah, Plain and Tall* (Harper) for the Newbery Medal. One of my children informed me rather pointedly that there are close to a hundred words for *snow* in Eskimo, implying that I, too, ought to be able to find precise, meaningful words of my own. However, *thank you* seems just right for this book that is as plain and simple as *thank you*. And because I have never forgotten my third-grade teacher's rule that every story must have a beginning, a middle, and an end—and I suppose a speech must follow the same rule—I would like to add my appreciation here for those people who have, in one way or another, had great influence on my beginnings as a writer.

Thank you, Craig Virden, for bringing out both

the worst and the best in me and for knowing that both parts translate into words. Thank you, Jane Yolen, for luring me into the world of children's literature. Every writer should have a loving reader who has the courage to write both "I love this" and "Ugh" on the same page. Thank you, Natalie Babbitt, for offering bare-boned advice and honest and true friendship. When I asked Natalie what I should say today, she replied, "Say anything. Just don't natter on." That is both advice *and* friendship. A child reader offered the same wisdom when he wrote, "Congratulations. I know you have to write a speech. Try, if you can, not to be boring." Last, thank you to my extended family at Harper & Row, particularly Charlotte Zolotow, who has in ways both wise and sly allowed and encouraged me to pull this story out into the light where I could see it well enough to write it.

I wanted to write a beautiful speech full of truths that would astonish you all, and I set about reading the writings of others, those who have won a medal and those who have not. After all, we are only a breath apart. The truths, I found, have all been told, spoken by thoughtful, articulate writers and lovers of children's literature. "Why is an idea always better in your head than on paper?" a small boy once asked me. Wise child. Edith Wharton, I told him, said the same thing when she wrote "I dream of an eagle, I give birth to a hummingbird." If that is the way of books, it is just as true of the writing of this speech, which is every bit as difficult to write as any book. With the fervent hope that there is not one thing wrong with a hummingbird, then, that is what you'll get—a hummingbird of a speech. It has also occurred to me that it would be unseemly to write a Newbery acceptance that is longer than the book for which the award is given.

My daughter, Emily, at age five said what is closest to what I feel now—children often do—when on the hottest of summer days she put on winter clothes to go out to play. "Why?" I asked her. "It's much too warm." "Because," she told me matter-of-factly, her hand on the door, "wearing these clothes makes me feel joyish." A child's truth. Wearing the clothes of the Newbery makes me feel joyish, too, though I'll admit the outfit is made up of layers, many of which are well worn, some new and unfamiliar, like gold lamé draped on a dime-store dummy. And although those who know me well know that I am uncomfortable talking about myself, except after sodium pentothal or several glasses of wine, I would like to tell you about the roots of this story, in the process of which you will probably know more about me than you care to know.

When I learned that I had won the Newbery, it was after lunch with friends, not my best time of day, even though my fortune cookie was the only one with a prophetic message. It said: "Your talents will soon be recognized." Honest it did. I will carry it with me always so that when I am in the middle of a book or a speech, where I am always convinced that I am tedious or dull or self-conscious, I will remember that once upon a time I was talented.

My best time of day as a writer—not as a parent—is between five-thirty and eight in the morning, when I make what at the time seem to me to be the most startling observations. The observations, mind you, that later as I write them become as common as the odd glass of water, the coffee dregs, the garbage of the day—those things, surprise or no surprise, that are what life and literature are made up of. The sunrise and I are close friends; we are well connected. Good word, *connection*—for if I feel connected to the sunrise, I am even more connected to childhood. Once when I was young, I had a dream that the sun did not rise because I had overslept. Ah, the wonderful self-centeredness that is allowed, that is *necessary* in childhood, suspicious in adulthood. Dare I admit that I have had the same dream as an adult? You bet I do. My daughter gave me permission when she exclaimed one day, "When are we grown up anyway?" When, indeed.

E. L. Konigsburg, writing in *Celebrating Children's Books* (Lothrop), confesses to the same thing after describing a trip to New York after winning the Newbery: "But because I retain this ability to see myself as the center of the universe, I can write for children. And because the adult part of me can see how absolutely ridiculous I am when I am doing it, my writings are readable." I wonder if there really is that adult part of me, for every morning as the sun comes up I crash downstairs, first one up, to clamp myself against the kitchen sink and watch the sun come up over the hills. It does not seem ridiculous. It is serious business.

At the moment that Dudley Carlson of the Newbery Committee told me of the award, I was articulate and adult—you can ask her. I was, however, at the same moment touched by a curious, childlike sense of immortality, much like one of my children who asked one day if I could please see to it that he be buried standing up, as if he might one day walk right out of the situation. When I said that I would probably die before him, he did not seem terribly perturbed. These thoughts of immortality surfaced later in the week when I was being interviewed. "What would you like written on your tombstone?" asked the interviewer. I leaned forward. "Do you mean I'm going to die?" I asked. I *think* I was kidding. Definitely the gold lamé part of the outfit. What I remember most, what fit best, was that as I spoke to Dudley and Liz Gordon and Charlotte Zolotow, our dog, Hilly, was nosing her dish around the floor, three hours ahead of time *as always*. My son Jamie was waiting for me to continue an absurd, ongoing nineteen-year-old game of who can touch whom last, which has no rules except that I lose and laugh about it and find myself lurking behind doors like a fool. My husband, Bob, was there where he had always been, and there was a red-breasted nuthatch on the bird feeder. I knew that if I called our oldest son, John, he would burst into tears of excitement. I did, and he did. And so did joyous Emily. And I thank them all, even the nuthatch who has been at the feeder ever since, for reminding me that it is the sturdy shoes that happily endure; those ground-gripper truths that reassure us that with the champagne comes tuna noodle surprise for dinner. The old dog is fed or she makes your life miserable; the familiar bank teller hands you a congratulatory flower the next morning and tells you that you're overdrawn—evidence of life, both the magic and the muck of it. After all, the muse whispers to me, you were a full-blown adult, a wife and mother, long before you ever became a writer. Just what is the magic—the literature or the life from which it grows?

*Sarah, Plain and Tall* grew out of these same experiences, what my mother used to call the heroics of a common life. When Julius Lester praises children's literature as the "literature that gives full attention to the ordinary," he echoes my parents' belief that it is the daily grace and dignity with which we survive that children most need and wish to know about in books. My parents believed in the truths of literature, and it was my mother who urged me to "read a book and find out who you are," for there are those of us who read or write to slip happily into the characters of those we'd like to be. It is, I believe, our way of getting to know the good and bad of us, rehearsing to be more humane, "revising our lives in our books," as John Gardner wrote, "so that we won't have to make the same mistakes again." My father and I played out daily scenes in the cloaks of the characters, engaging in extended plots that we changed as we wished. More rehearsal. It was a safe way to bump up against life, and exciting because my father always invited questions and disagreement. Our plots could make you cry, and I don't mean tears of joy. His enthusiasm—coupled with my mother's incredible tolerance for the eccentricities and subtleties of people, particularly children—meant that I could risk being a rascal. And I was, like the horse Jack in *Sarah, Plain and Tall*. It is the essence of my parents' acceptance reflected in the character of Anna and Caleb's father when he complains that Jack was feisty in town. "'Rascal,' murmured Papa, smiling, because no matter what Jack did Papa loved him."

My mother told me early on about the real Sarah, who came from the coast of Maine to the prairie to become a wife and mother to a close family member. My mother remembered her fondly. "Is that real?" demanded a schoolchild. "Just what are the facts?" This is the question most asked by children, I suppose because part of childhood is concerned with sorting out the facts from the fiction, both truths of life. Recently in Pittsburgh I was confronted by some heretofore unknown facts. While reading some children's comments, I saw the following. Question: What is the Newbery medal? Answer: It is for telling the best joke. It looks like a tomato. It *is* a tomato. Question: Who is Patricia MacLachlan? Answer: She is famous because she had a baby on the Brooklyn Bridge.

I, too, am still trying to sort out facts for myself, though with little luck. "I've noticed," said a friend recently, "that you don't pay much attention to facts. They are not," she added, "of great importance to you." I confess to this. Facts are like an oil painting which begins with a figure and soon succumbs to layers of paint so that the original is lost underneath. Facts are, for me, close to what the writer Harriet Doerr describes as memories in *Stones for Ibarra* (Viking), when she writes that "memories are like corks left out of bottles. They swell. They no longer fit." I will believe anything, fact or fiction, if it's written or told well, as Jane Yolen will tell you. She called me once to read a passage she was writing about a dragon giving birth, laying its eggs in the sand. "Tell me if this works for you," she said. After she read I was incredulous. "I didn't know dragons laid eggs," I said. "I thought they had live young." There was silence. "Patty," she said, "dragons are imaginary." Oh. "It works," I muttered.

So the fact of Sarah was there for years, though

the book began, as books often do, when the past stepped on the heels of the present, or backward, when something *now* tapped something *then*. Two of my children began to prepare to leave home for college, first one, then the other. But before they left, my parents took us on a trip west to the prairie, where they and I had been born. It was a gift for all of us, for the children to see a land they had never seen, to know family they had never met, to stand on the vast North Dakota farm where my father had been born in a sod house and, as Anna observes, "the prairie reached out and touched the places where the sky came down." Maya Angelou said recently that when Thomas Wolfe said you can't go home again, he was right. But he was also wrong, for you can't really ever leave either. It was a startling connection from the past to open the door of the granary, the only building still standing, and find a gopher filling his cheeks with grain.

But mostly it was an important and poignant connection for my mother who was, because of

Alzheimer's disease, beginning to lose her memory. How splendid if memories swell like corks out of a bottle! How cruel when they diminish and disappear. First there is no more present. Then there is no past. At last there are no more words. "Words, words, words," complained a frustrated young writer in a letter to me. "Is that all writers have?" Yes and no. Sarah speaks for me and my mother, for whom there are few words left, when she writes in the book: "My brother William is a fisherman, and he tells me that when he is in the middle of a fogbound sea the water is a color for which there is no name." This is my favorite sentence in the book, and I know why. It is my attempt to say what I have always thought and only been able to say in Sarah's voice: that words are limiting, an odd thing for a writer to say. There is an entire world, complex and layered and full, behind each word or between words, that is often present but not spoken. And it is often what is left unsaid that shapes and empowers a moment, an experience, a book. Or a life.

Actors know this. Musicians know it, too.

When I began *Sarah*, I wished for several things and was granted something unexpected. Most of all I wished to write my mother's story with spaces, like the prairie, with silences that could say what words could not. I began the story as a picture book, and it is clear to me that I wanted to wrap the land and the people as tightly as I could and hand this small piece of my mother's past to her in a package as perfect as Anna's sea stone, as Sarah's sea. But books, like children, grow and change, borrowing bits and pieces of the lives of others to help make them who and what they are. And in the end we are all there, my mother, my father, my husband, my children, and me. We gave my mother better than a piece of her past. We gave her the same that Anna and Caleb and Sarah and Jacob received—a family.

One day when my mother still had words in her, we went for a drive in the country. We talked. Suddenly, my mother reached out to touch my arm. "Now who are you?" she asked. "I am your daughter," I said. "Ah," she said, leaning back and smiling, "then isn't it nice that I like you."

Now I hope you can see why I am enormously pleased and honored to accept this award for this book. Thank you.

## SARAH, PLAIN AND TALL
### by Patricia MacLachlan
### Common Core–aligned Discussion Guide

Before Reading

1. Create a class bulletin board or collage depicting images of frontier life in the 1900s. In your visual representation include pictures of houses, families, transportation, clothing, food, working conditions, schooling, and so forth. Participate in a class discussion about the photos. What do you find most intriguing about this time? What might have been most challenging about living on the frontier during the 1900s?

2. Mail-order brides (or grooms) were common during this time in remote territories. Read about this practice then discuss why it might have been common.

CCSS: SL.3.1, SL.4.1, SL.5.1

Discussion Questions

1. Anna and Caleb's mother dies giving birth to Caleb. Describe the impact her loss has on both Anna and Caleb and on their father. Why do both Anna and Caleb feel guilty?

2. Both Caleb and Anna long for their mother. Explain how the author shows readers that Caleb and Anna miss her. Use examples from the story to support your answer. What words or phrases does the author use to make readers sympathize with Caleb and Anna?

3. Caleb says, "Papa doesn't sing anymore." What does this statement reveal about Papa? Why does Anna ask if Sarah sings? How do Anna and Caleb respond when they learn that Sarah does sing? What themes in the story does this question address?

4. Describe the setting of the story. What was daily life like for the family? Discuss how their daily routine changes once Sarah arrives. In what way is life on the frontier different for Sarah?

5. How does Papa reveal to Anna and Caleb that he has written to Sarah? Is he hesitant about his decision? Why or why not? What response do Anna and Caleb have to his announcement?

6. Who is Sarah and how does she come to live with the family? What do Caleb and Anna think of her? Find passages in the story that illustrate their feelings. Do Caleb and Anna want her to stay? What fear do they have? How does the author illustrate their fear? Use evidence from the story to support your answers.

7. How does the author describe Sarah? Is she a likable character? Describe how she fits in with the family. How does Caleb know that she plans to stay? Support your answers with evidence from the story.

8. The author does not reveal a great deal about Sarah's former life. What does she state explicitly about Sarah's past? What can you infer? Use evidence from the story to support your answers.

9. Imagery is when the author uses language that

appeals to the senses. Sometimes to create vivid scenes, authors use similes and metaphors. Review the definition of both literary terms and find examples of each in the story. Discuss the effect these literary devices have on the story.

10. Compare and contrast Anna's and Caleb's attitudes toward having Sarah stay with them. How does the author keep the reader guessing as to whether Sarah will stay or whether she will return to the east?

11. Sarah indicates that she loves and misses the sea. What evidence can you find in the story that shows her affection for the sea? Should Sarah have left her brother? Why or why not?

12. Identify one character and describe how that person changes as the story develops. Describe one event that impacts the character and discuss how this event contributes to the character's growth.

CCSS: SL.3.1, SL.4.1, SL.5.1, RL.3.1, RL.4.1, RL.5.1, RL.3.3, RL.4.3, RL.5.3, RL.3.4, RL.4.4, RL.5.4

Extension Activities

1. Music is a part of the fabric of every culture and time period. Read about music in the 1900s. What kinds of songs and musical instruments were popular for frontier families? Pretend you are either Caleb or Anna and write a song or poem about life on the frontier. Share your piece in a small group or before the class.

2. Pair up with a classmate and make two collages. One collage should depict life on the frontier in the 1900s. The other should depict life in the Northeastern part of the country near the sea in the same time period. Share your work with the class and discuss the similarities and differences represented in your visual presentations.

3. Assume the role of Anna or Caleb and write two diary entries. The first entry should describe your first impression of Sarah; the second should describe your feelings after she has been with the family for some time.

4. Imagine that you are Sarah or her brother.

Partner with a classmate who takes on the alternate role and exchange letters in which you talk about your new life. What questions do you have for the other? What dreams do you have for yourself and for your sibling?

5. Working in small groups, brainstorm a scene that you could add to the story that would give readers a deeper understanding of any one character. Write the scene and draw an illustration to accompany it. Share it with the class.

6. Research the weather on the frontier and on the Maine coastline. Compare and contrast the weather in the two geographical regions. Where would you prefer to spend winter and why? Where would you prefer to spend summer and why? Draw a picture of your favorite season in one of the two regions, and share it with the class.

CCSS: W.3.3, W.4.3, W.5.3, SL.3.1, SL.4.1, SL.5.1, W.3.7, W.4.7, W.5.7

Teaching guide created by Pam B. Cole, Associate Dean and Professor of English Education and Literacy, Kennesaw State University, Kennesaw, GA.

# Suggested Reading List

Bunting, Eve. *The Summer of Riley*. New York: HarperCollins Publishers, 2001.

Cushman, Karen. *The Ballard of Lucy Whipple*. Boston: Houghton Mifflin Harcourt, 1996.

Fritz, Jean. *The Cabin Faced West*. New York: Penguin Group (USA), 1958.

Harvey, Brett. *My Prairie Year: Based on the Diary of Elenore Plaisted*. New York: Holiday House, Inc.,1988.

Hermes, Patricia. *Westward to Home: Joshua's Oregon Trail Diary*. New York: Scholastic, Inc., 2001.

Hest, Amy. *Remembering Mrs. Rossi*. Boston: Candlewick Press, 2007.

Kalman, Bobbie. *Historic Communities Series: A Child's Day*. New York: Crabtree Publishing Company, 1993

Kamma, Anne. *If You Were a Pioneer on the Prairie*. New York: Scholastic, Inc., 2003.

McMullan, Kate. *A Fine Start: Meg's Prairie Diary*. New York: Scholastic, Inc., 2003.

Nixon, Joan Lowery. *The Orphan Train Adventures Series #1: A Family Apart*. New York: Random House, Children's Books, 1987.

Shaw, Janet. *American Girl Collection Series: Kirsten #1: Meet Kirsten*. Madison: American Girl Publishing, 1986.

Wilder, Laura Ingalls. *Farmer Boy*. New York: HarperCollins Publishers, 1953.

Wilder, Laura Ingalls. *Little House in the Big Woods*. New York: HarperCollins Publishers, 1953.

Wiles, Deborah. *Each Little Bird That Sings*. Boston: Houghton Mifflin Harcourt, 2005.

Turn the page for an excerpt from the
second book in the *Sarah, Plain and Tall*
series by Patricia MacLachlan

# Skylark

## 1

"Stand on that stump, Caleb. Anna, you next to him. That will be a good family picture."

Joshua, the photographer, looked through his big camera at us as we stood on the porch squinting in the sunlight. Caleb wore a white shirt, his hair combed slick to his head, Sarah in a white dress, Papa looking hot and uneasy in his suit. The lace at my neck itched in the summer heat. We had to be still for so long that Caleb began to whistle softly, making Sarah smile.

Far off in the distance the dogs, Nick and Lottie, walked slowly through the dry prairie grass. They walked past the cow pond nearly empty of water, past the wagon, past the chickens in the yard. Nick saw us first, then Lottie, and they began to run. Caleb looked sideways at me as they jumped the fence and ran to us, running up to stand between Sarah and Papa as if they wanted to be in the picture, too. We tried not to laugh, but Sarah couldn't help it. She looked up at Papa and he smiled down at her. And Joshua took the picture of us all laughing, Papa smiling at Sarah.

Joshua laughed, too.

"Your aunts will like that picture," he said to Sarah.

Sarah fanned herself.

"They hardly know what I look like anymore," she said softly. "I hardly know what *they* look like anymore."

I looked at Caleb. I knew Caleb didn't like to think about Sarah and her aunts and her brother and the sea she had left behind.

"It's Maine you came from, isn't it?" said Joshua.

"Yes," said Sarah.

"She lives *here* now," said Caleb loudly.

Papa put his hand on Caleb's head.

"That she does," said Joshua, smiling.

He turned and looked out over the cornfield, the plants so dry they rattled in the wind.

"But I bet Maine is green," Joshua said in a low voice. He looked out over the land with a faraway look, as if he were somewhere else. "We sure could use rain. I remember a long time ago, you remember it, Jacob. The water dried up, the fields so dry that the leaves fell like dust. And then the winds came. My grandfather packed up his family and left."

"Did he come back?" asked Caleb.

Joshua turned.

"No," he said, "he never came back."

Joshua packed up the last of his things and got up in his wagon.

Papa looked at Sarah.

"It will rain," he said.

We watched the wagon go off down the road.

"It will rain," Papa repeated softly.